To Franje, my sister-in-law, who is now in heaven.
Thank you for being Demi's inspiration and our matchmaker.

Valentines 2023

To Lila I.
I believe
in you
Love
Mamama

BRONCO AND FRIENDS: MISSION POSSIBLE

All Scripture quotations are taken from the ESV® Bible
(The Holy Bible, English Standard Version®), copyright © 2001
by Crossway, a publishing ministry of Good News Publishers.
Used by permission. All rights reserved.

Text and illustrations copyright © 2022 by Timothy R. Tebow

All rights reserved.

Published in the United States by WaterBrook, an imprint of
Random House, a division of Penguin Random House LLC.

WATERBROOK® and its deer colophon are registered
trademarks of Penguin Random House LLC.

ISBN 978-0-593-23206-4
Ebook ISBN 978-0-593-23207-1

The Library of Congress catalog record is available at
https://lccn.loc.gov/2020052170.

Printed in China

waterbrookmultnomah.com

10 9 8 7 6 5 4 3 2 1

First Edition

Cover and interior illustrations by Jane Chapman
Book and cover design by Patrice Sheridan,
    based on the design by Mia Johnson

SPECIAL SALES Most WaterBrook books are available at
special quantity discounts when purchased in bulk by corporations,
organizations, and special-interest groups. Custom imprinting or
excerpting can also be done to fit special needs. For information,
please email specialmarketscms@penguinrandomhouse.com.

BRONCO AND FRIENDS

Mission Possible

Tim Tebow

with A. J. Gregory

Illustrated by Jane Chapman

WATERBROOK

Ahh!

Bronco stretched out under the warm sun. It was always fun to hang out with old friends, even though they weren't the best at sharing their treats.

Chunk beamed with pride.
"Look what I made!"

"My favorite,"
Paris howled.

"It's cake!" Kobe barked, spilling
the secret. "Made with honey."

"Save some for me!" Bronco yelped.

The pooches gobbled up the scrumptious honey cake,
but their feast was cut short by some unwelcome visitors.

"Stop! Don't eat that!" Kobe yelled at Paris.

"Help! Get them off of me!" Chunk cried.
"They make me itch like crazy."

"Quick! Run for cover!" Bronco bellowed, diving
into the bushes. He cowered and covered his
eyes as something flew straight toward him.
"Nooooo!"

To Bronco's horror, a bee touched down right on his tail. "Go away!" he yelped.

Flexing her deepest muscles, the bee hummed, "Help me!" But Bronco was too scared to listen.

He sped away, through the trail between the trees, down the hill, and way out into the farmer's field.

"ACHOOOO!"

Alexis groaned, then struggled to her feet and shook herself. "What just happened?"

Bronco whimpered, panting wildly. "I'm scared of bees, and I can't get this thing off me!"

Unexpectedly, the bee released her grip and started zigzagging around Bronco's face.

Alexis scrunched her forehead and leaned in closer. "I think it's trying to tell us something!"

"Oh?" Bronco peered at the bee.

"I need your help!" the bee bumbled. "My name is Phoebe. My family and I were stolen from the beekeeper who loves and cares for us. I was the only bee to escape. Will you help me find my family?"

Why would I help a bunch of bees I don't even know? Bronco thought. *They've never done anything for me.*

"Please?" Phoebe begged. "I don't know what else to do!"

Suddenly, Bronco remembered a poem
his mother used to read to him.

We all will have choices,
some great and some small,
to help someone who
can't help us at all.

And we must decide
to sit or stand tall.
Will you turn away
or say yes to the call?

Bronco knew what he needed to do. "Of course we'll help you, Phoebe. But we're going to need a bigger team for the job."

Bronco whistled so loudly, the
trees shook. Chelsie pounced
over the hill with Ethan perched
on her ear. "Hello, friends!"

Bronco revealed the bee-rescue mission to Chelsie and Ethan. They were eager to help.

"What's the last thing you remember?" Chelsie asked Phoebe.

"Splashing!" buzzed the bee. "Like someone was walking through water."

"The stream!" shouted Ethan. "I saw it when I was hopping along the branches on a tree down there."

The five friends raced toward the ravine.

Which way do we go? Bronco wondered. He sniffed around. "Left!" he shouted and took off along the southern edge.

Paws and hooves raced through the woods as Phoebe whirred her wings against the wind.

"I think we're close," Phoebe buzzed. "I can smell my cousins!"

Suddenly, Ethan tugged on Chelsie's ear.

"What's the matter, Ethan?"

Ethan clenched Chelsie's fur with a mighty grip.
"I think—I think I hear a lawn mower!"

Phoebe froze in flight. "I don't like those things!"

"ACHOOo!"

Alexis rubbed her eyes.

"I'll check it out," Bronco offered. The brave pup disappeared into a clump of bushes. Soon after, his friends heard loud barking. "It's not a lawn mower. It's the bees! I found them."

"Phew!" buzzed Phoebe.

The friends hurtled after Bronco's voice.
"There's the hive!" Phoebe cried.

Phoebe swooped down to the entrance of the
bee box. "We're here to rescue you!"

A chorus of wild buzzing exploded. Bronco and friends looked at one another in confusion.

"They won't leave without the queen," Phoebe explained. "But she's too afraid!"

The furry friends leapt into the back of the truck. Alexis peered into the hole. "Miss Queen? We're here to help. You're not safe here."

The queen bee trembled. "But what if we don't make it?"

"We believe in you!" Bronco barked.

Chelsie smiled encouragingly. "Your family is counting on you to lead them home."

"You have work to do, Miss Queen," Ethan chirped. "And you can't do it here."

Bronco's ears twitched. "Hurry! I think someone's coming."

Miss Queen took a deep breath. "Okay, I can do this." She revved up her wings and commanded the colony, "Move out!"

A buzzing cloud of yellow and black swarmed out of the box.

"Follow us!" Phoebe instructed.

"Run!" Bronco yelled.

As the friends approached the ravine,
they stopped to catch their breath.

"Thank you for saving us!" Miss Queen exclaimed.
"We can find our way back from here!"

"It takes a team to make a mission work!" Bronco barked proudly.

"Woof! Woof! Woof!"

Chunk, Kobe, and Paris pounced onto the path. "Bronco! Where have you been?"

Bronco and his friends slept well that night. They had found the courage to do what was right, not what was easy.

And the bees? Well, they had their own missions to complete.

It might be easier to do nothing at all,
but God has asked you to answer the call.

"Let each of you look not only to
his own interests, but also to
the interests of others."

Philippians 2:4